This book belongs to

....

ROW, ROW, ROW YOUR BOAT

-- AND OTHER RHYMES --

Illustrated by Dawn Machell

DUCKTAIL

make believe ideas

INCY WINCY SPIDER

climbed up the waterspout.
Down came the RAIN
and washed the spider out.

Out came the SUNSHINE and dried up all the RAIN, and INCY WINCY SPIDER climbed up the spout again.

HEY DIDDLE DIDDLE, the CAT and the fiddle,

the COW jumped over the MOON.

The little DOG laughed
to see such fun,

and the DISH ran away
with the SPOON.

One for the MASTER,
one for the DAME,

and one for the little BOY who lives down the LANE.

I SEE the MOON
and the MOON sees me.

God bless the **MOON**
and **GOD** bless me!

TWINKLE, TWINKLE, little STAR, how I wonder what YOU are.

?

Up above the
WORLD
so high,

like a
DIAMOND
in the sky.

Twinkle, twinkle,
little STAR,
how I wonder what you are.

ROW, ROW, ROW YOUR BOAT,

gently down the STREAM,

MERRILY, MERRILY,
MERRILY, MERRILY,
life is but a DREAM.

WEE WILLIE WINKIE
runs through the TOWN,
UPSTAIRS and downstairs
in his NIGHTGOWN.

Tapping at the WINDOW and CRYING through the lock, "Are all the CHILDREN in their BEDS? It's past EIGHT o'clock!"

HICKORY DICKORY DOCK,

the MOUSE ran up the CLOCK.

The CLOCK struck ONE,

the **MOUSE** ran

DOWN,

HICKORY

DICKORY

DOCK.

PAT-A-CAKE, PAT-A-CAKE, BAKER'S man.

BAKE me a CAKE as FAST as you can.

PAT it and **PRICK** it and **mark** it with **B,**

and **put** it in the **OVEN** for **BABY** and **me.**

TEDDY BEAR, TEDDY BEAR, TURN AROUND.

Teddy Bear, Teddy Bear, **TOUCH the GROUND.**

Teddy Bear, Teddy Bear, **GO UPSTAIRS.**

Teddy Bear, Teddy Bear, say your **PRAYERS**.

Teddy Bear, Teddy Bear, **TURN OFF** the light.

Teddy Bear, Teddy Bear, **SAY GOODNIGHT**.